Sandy Hill Elementary School
Glasgow Road
Cambridge, Maryland

DID YOU SEE WHAT I SAID?

WRITTEN & ILLUSTRATED
BY SHAN ELLENTUCK

Sandy Hill Elementary School
Glasgow Road
Cambridge, Maryland

Doubleday & Company, Inc.   Garden City, New York

Library of Congress Catalog Card Number AC 67-10011
Copyright © 1967 by Merna Ellentuck
All Rights Reserved
Printed in the United States of America
9 8 7 6 5 4 3 2

For Shari, Lori and Amy
And for Harriet

Miss Pandora Parker was a terrible
busybody. She loved to talk about
people—

and she was always sticking her
nose in somebody's business.

Did you SEE what I said?

I SAID—

"She was always sticking her nose
in somebody's business!"

And what tall tales Miss Parker told!
She didn't exactly lie—but she
certainly painted things bigger than
life.

Did you SEE what I said?

"She certainly painted things
bigger than life!"

Late one afternoon
Miss Parker noticed
a very peculiar
wagon parked at the
edge of the woods.

It was like a little house on wheels
with a crooked chimney and flapping
shutters on the tiny windows.
Of course she rushed right over to
have a closer look. She was beside
herself with curiosity.

Did you SEE what I said?

"She was beside herself
with curiosity!"

There was no one in sight and not much to see except for a bit of smoke huffing and puffing out of the chimney. BUT when Miss Parker pressed her ear to the door there were some very interesting noises indeed! There was a rattling and banging. There was a bumping and thumping. And SOMETHING inside was screeching and screaming!

"Something's wrong! Something's dreadfully wrong!" cried Miss Parker as she hurried back uptown. Her voice was worried, but really, she was tickled pink to have something new to talk about!

Did you SEE what I said?

"She was tickled pink to have something
new to talk about!"

First she ran in to tell the butcher
about the mysterious wagon.
"Nonsense!" said the butcher.
"Oh, it isn't nonsense," whispered
Miss Parker. "I heard loud rattling
and banging, screeching and screaming.
THERE MUST BE SOMETHING
LARGE AND FIERCE LOCKED
UP IN THAT WAGON!"

Then Miss Parker
hurried to the bakery.
The butcher was right
behind her.

When he heard her story, the baker
laughed out loud.

"Don't laugh!" Miss Parker warned
him. "There's smoke coming out of
that wagon as though SOMETHING
INSIDE IS BREATHING FIRE!"

The garbageman stuck his head in
the door. "Who's breathing fire?"
he asked.

"What?"

"Where?"

In frightened whispers the butcher and the baker told the garbageman about the strange THING.

"And there was an awful thumping noise," added Miss Parker, "as if *something* were trying to get out. It wouldn't surprise me a bit if there was A DRAGON IN THAT WAGON!"

"A dragon in the wagon?" cried the garbageman. "My dear Miss Parker, you must have rocks in your head!"

Did you SEE what he said?

He SAID—
"You must have rocks
in your head!"

"If you don't believe me," shouted Miss
Parker, "listen!"
Sure enough, there was the faraway
sound of thumping and bumping and—
suddenly—a dreadful screech filled
the air.
"Help!" yelled the garbageman, "Danger!
Dragon!" And he ran lickety-split
down the street, waving his arms.

Soon the street was full of frightened
people, running every which way. Everybody was in a terrible stew.

Did you SEE what I said?

"Everybody was in a terrible stew!"

The butcher, waving his longest knife,
led the crowd toward the mystery wagon.
Behind him came the baker with a roll-
ing pin. The garbageman had a broom.

Miss Parker grabbed a ball of string.
"You knock him down," she called,
"and I'll tie him up!"
All of them were pretending to be
brave—but every last one of them
was scared stiff.

Did you SEE what I said?

"Every   last   one   of   them

was   scared   STIFF!''

The butcher banged on the door of the
wagon. "We've come for the dragon!"
he shouted. Slowly the shutters swung
open and a sleepy-looking gentleman
popped his head out.

"The dragon?" said the gentleman, with
a yawn. "What dragon? Gracious—have
you all lost your heads?"

Did you SEE what he said?

"Gracious—have you all lost your heads?"

"This is NO joke!" growled the garbage-man, shaking his broom.

The gentleman was wide awake now. "Wait a minute!" he cried. "I don't have any such thing in here. See for yourselves!"

The door flew open and everyone crowded around to look inside. Somebody gasped. Somebody giggled. Soon the whole crowd was roaring with laughter.

"Look, Miss Parker," laughed the butcher, pointing to the potbellied stove. "THAT's what's making your dragon smoke!"
"And there's your rattling, banging, screeching and screaming!" howled the baker, pointing to the eight cats, two parrots and the very large yellow dog.

The dog, pleased to see all the
people, began wagging his tail—
bump, bump, bump on the floor.
"And THAT is your dreadful dragon
thumping!" giggled the garbageman,
wiping the tears from his eyes.
"Miss Parker," he said, "I'm
afraid you've made monkeys out
of us all!"

Did you SEE what he said?

"I'm afraid you've made
monkeys out of us all!"

Miss Parker hung her head.
"I'm sorry," she said to the
gentleman from the wagon.
"I'm sorry," she said to the
baker, the butcher, the
garbageman and
everyone in the
crowd. "I'm so
ashamed," she
said, "I wish I
could sink right
into the ground!"

Did
you
SEE
what
she
said?